Usborne

Dragons
Magic Painting
Book

Illustrated by
Camilla Garofano

Designed by Brenda Cole

To stop water from
seeping through to the next
page, unfold the flap at the
back of the book and place
it under the page you're
about to work on.

Dip the brush into
water, then brush
it across the black
patterns within each
shape to see the paint
magically appear.